WITHDRAWN

FOR Hilary
S.C.

FOR Sue, Jana, & Graham
J.K.

Text copyright © 1997 by Sheridan Cain
Illustrations copyright © 1997 by Jo Kelly
All rights reserved.
CIP Data is available.
Published in the United States 1998
by Dutton Children's Books,
a member of Penguin Putnam Inc.
375 Hudson Street, New York, New York 10014
Originally published in Great Britain 1997
by Magi Publications, London
Typography by Ellen M. Lucaire
Printed in Belgium
First American Edition
ISBN 0-525-45963-4
2 4 6 8 10 9 7 5 3 1

Why So Sad, Brown Rabbit?

BY

Sheridan Cain

ILLUSTRATED BY

Jo Kelly

Dutton Children's Books
New York

Spring had come at last. All the rabbits were playing Hop, Skip, and Jump around the meadow. But watching from the edge, with his ears all droopy, sat Brown Rabbit.

"Why so sad, Brown Rabbit?" asked Gray Mouse. "It's a lovely day."

"I wish I could hop, skip, and jump, too," said Brown Rabbit, "but I'm too old to play games."

"If only you had a family," said Gray Mouse. "Then you could teach your *children* to play games. That would be just as much fun."

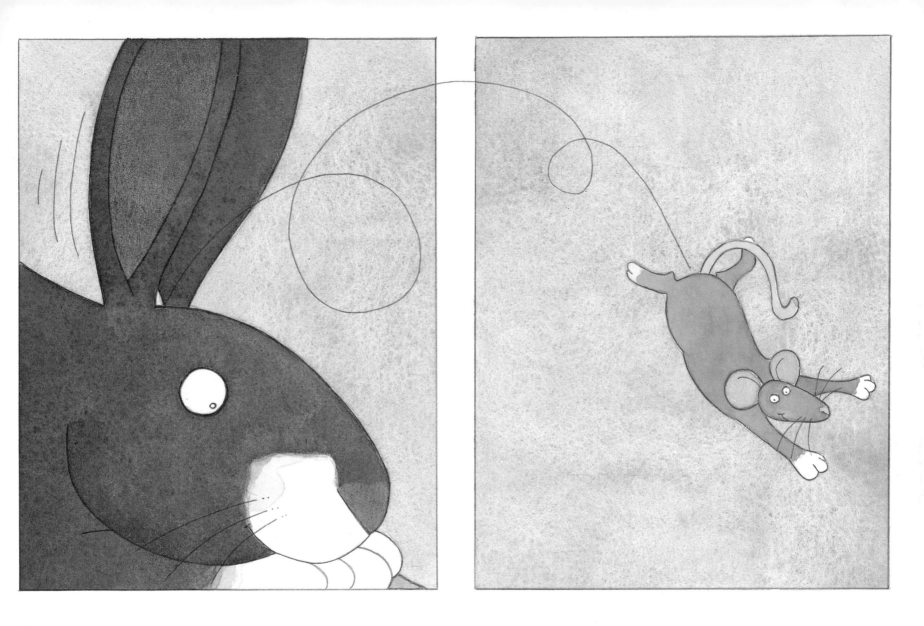

Brown Rabbit's spirits lifted and so did his ears,
sending Gray Mouse flying.

"That's a wonderful idea," said Brown Rabbit, helping
the little mouse to his feet. "I must find a wife at once."

Brown Rabbit set off that very day. He hopped across fields...

and he hopped through woods...

and he hopped over hills, but he soon discovered
that a wife wasn't an easy thing to find.

Brown Rabbit was tired,
and his feet were sore.

He stopped by a barn
and rested on a pile of hay.

Very soon, he was fast asleep.

Suddenly, Brown Rabbit woke
with a start—*what was wrong?*

Something was wiggling
and jiggling under the hay.

He looked down and saw three eggs.

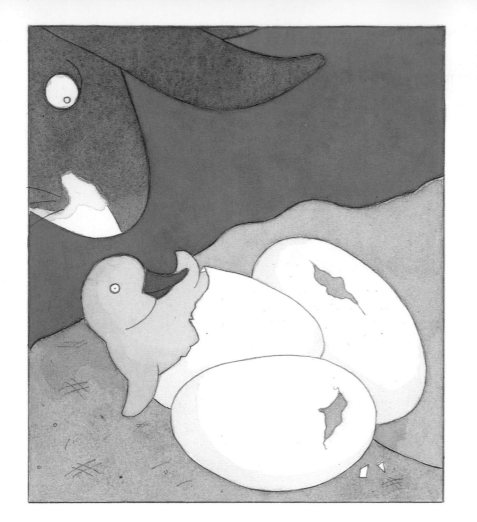

As Brown Rabbit watched, one of the eggs began to crack.
A tiny beak appeared, then a tiny wet head. The egg fell apart,
and out stepped a little duckling.
There was another crack, and another...

. . . and now there were three little ducklings,
all standing in a row.
   "Mama!" they quacked, looking straight at Brown Rabbit.
   "Oh dear. I'm not your mama," said Brown Rabbit in dismay.
But it was no good.
   "MAMA, MAMA," they quacked again.

"Don't worry, little ducklings," said Brown Rabbit.
"I'll help you find your mama."
   He set off toward the farmyard, and the ducklings waddled after him.

Very soon they met Porker Pig.

"Hello," said Brown Rabbit. "These little fellows have lost their mama. Have you seen her?"

"No ducks around here," snorted Porker, and without another word, she went on eating her breakfast.

Brown Rabbit thumped his feet. He thought Porker
was not helpful at all, so he hopped away toward the pond.
"MAMA!" cried the ducklings, trying to keep up with him.

Very soon they met White Swan.

"Hello," said Brown Rabbit. "These little fellows want their mama. Have you seen her?"

"Certainly not!" hissed White Swan. "This is my pond. I do not share it with noisy, messy, splashing ducks." He turned his back on Brown Rabbit and the little ducklings and glided silently away.

"Thanks for nothing," said Brown Rabbit angrily.
He hopped on into the farmyard, and the ducklings
hurried along behind him.

"MAMA!" they cried. "Wait for us!"

Brown Rabbit slowed down so they could keep up.

Right in front of him was Cackly Hen.

"Hello," said Brown Rabbit. "These little fellows need
their mama. Have you seen her anywhere?"

"*Cluck, cluck*, you are out of luck," said Cackly, pecking
at some corn. "All the ducks flew south yesterday."

Brown Rabbit sat down.

"What am I going to do?" he said miserably. He looked at the three sad, little faces. "You're all alone, just like me."

"MAMA!" the ducklings cried and snuggled up close.

Brown Rabbit suddenly felt better.
"How about a game?" he said. "That will cheer you up."
The little ducklings' faces lit up, so Brown Rabbit taught them . . .

how to hop . . .

and how to skip . . .

and how to jump.

What fun they had!

"MAMA!" cried the ducklings
in excitement. "MAMA!"
     "Oh, please don't call me Mama,"
said Brown Rabbit.

"PAPA!" cried the ducklings. "PAPA!"
Brown Rabbit smiled.
"Hurray!" cheered Gray Mouse.
"You've found your family at last!"